Ming Goes to School

Written by Deirdre Sullivan
Illustrated by Maja Löfdahl

Sky Pony Press
New York

For Daisy, Lila, Tess, and CeCe, you were all worth waiting for. —D. S.

To Fay, Alma, and Edith, and to their 婆婆 —M. L.

Sky Pony Press books may be purchased in bulk at special discounts for sales promotion, corporate gifts, fund-raising, or educational purposes. Special editions can also be created to specifications. For details, contact the Special Sales Department, Sky Pony Press, 307 West 36th Street, 11th Floor, New York, NY 10018 or info@skyhorsepublishing.com.

Sky Pony® is a registered trademark of Skyhorse Publishing, Inc.®, a Delaware corporation.

Visit our website at www.skyponypress.com.

10 9 8 7 6 5 4 3 2

Manufactured in China, June 2016
This product conforms to CPSIA 2008

Library of Congress Cataloging-in-Publication Data is available on file.

Cover design by Sarah Brody
Cover illustration credit Maja Löfdahl Green

Print ISBN: 978-1-5107-0050-5
Ebook ISBN: 978-1-5107-0055-0

Thank you to Julie Matysik at Sky Pony Press for believing in Ming.

Ming goes to school.

It's where she learns to say hello . . .

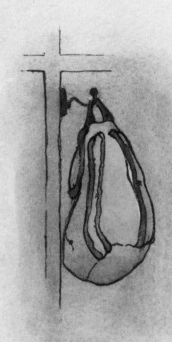

and good-bye.

It's where she meets new friends . . .

and introduces the old.

It's where magic fairy castles
are built from sticks . . .

and growing up takes time.

It's where she giggles . . .

and rests.

It's where she hosts pinkie-lifting tea parties . . .

and pretends to walk the plank.

It's where she squirms . . .

and traces, glitters,
and glues.

It's where all things . . .

are worth waiting for.

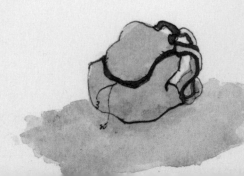

E